Nothing!

Nothing!

Yasmeen Ismail

BLOOMSBURY
LONDON OXFORD NEW YORK NEW DELHI SYDNEY

"Lila,
have you put your
shoes on yet?"

"Lila?"

"Lila, what *are* you doing?"

Nothing...

I'll fight this fearsome beastie
and soon he will regret
not giving up much sooner to
become my faithful pet . . .

"Lila, have you got
your **coat** on?

Grandpa will
be waiting!"

"What's going **on**
over there?"

FLIP and spring and ZOOM and tumble,

"OK, let's get going . . ."

Take the Train!

"Oh, Lila, what are you doing to that biscuit?"

Nothing...

RARRR-RRR!

Giants are the LOUDEST of all.

We're BIG and strong and very tall.

Fee – Fi – Fo and Fum!

You'd better hide before I come.

"Lila . . .

LILA!
Slow down!

What are
you *doing*?"

Nothing...

I am the queen of super speed!

Nothing can stop these noble steeds.

I'll CRASH down mountains and tear through trees!

You'll NEVER catch up with meeeee . . .

"Lila, look at you!
Are you getting taller?"

"What have you been doing
since I last saw you?"

Nothing...

I'm very busy all the time,

with things to see and trees to climb.

Up and up, right to the sky,

to wave at birds,
      as they *fly* by.

"Who are you waving to, Lila?"

"Lila?"

Oh, Grandpa,
　can't you *see*?
I was **sat**
　　up in that **tree** . . .

And like the birds, I'll *fly* away . . .

I don't suppose you could follow me?

Watch out, Lila! Here I come!
I too can play pretend!
There's really **nothing** to it . . .

It's SO much better with a friend!

For Lila
(Max and Spiderman)

Bloomsbury Publishing, London, Oxford, New York, New Delhi and Sydney

First published in Great Britain in 2016 by Bloomsbury Publishing Plc
50 Bedford Square, London, WC1B 3DP

Text and illustrations copyright © Yasmeen Ismail 2016
The moral rights of the author/illustrator have been asserted

A CIP catalogue record for this book is available from the British Library

ISBN 978 1 4088 7335 9 (HB)
ISBN 978 1 4088 7336 6 (PB)
ISBN 978 1 4088 7334 2 (eBook)

Printed in China by Leo Paper Products, Heshan, Guangdong

1 3 5 7 9 10 8 6 4 2

www.bloomsbury.com

BLOOMSBURY is a registered trademark of Bloomsbury Publishing Plc